Airplanes

Soaring! Diving! Turning!

by **Patricia Hubbell**
illustrated by **Megan Halsey**
and **Sean Addy**

Marshall Cavendish Children

For Capt. Wm. T. Halsey, Dad —M.H.

To Dad and Wayne for giving me the space to create —S.A.

Marshall Cavendish Corporation, 99 White Plains Road,
Tarrytown, NY 10591
www.marshallcavendish.us/kids

Library of Congress Cataloging-in-Publication Data
Hubbell, Patricia.
Airplanes : soaring! diving! turning! / by Patricia Hubbell;
illustrated by Megan Halsey and Sean Addy. — 1st ed.
p. cm.
Summary: Illustrations and rhyming text celebrate different
kinds of airplanes and what they can do.
ISBN 978-0-7614-5388-8
[1. Airplanes—Fiction. 2. Stories in rhyme.] I. Halsey, Megan, ill.
II. Addy, Sean, ill. III. Title.
PZ8.3.H848Ai 2008
[E]—dc22
2007011721

The text of this book is set in Nobel.

The illustrations are rendered in clip art, etchings, original drawings, and maps.

Book design by Virginia Pope

Editor: Margery Cuyler

Printed in Malaysia
First edition
1 3 5 6 4 2

Marshall Cavendish
Children

Down the runway!
Up they rise!

Night
and day,

planes cross the skies.

Cargo planes have lots of room.

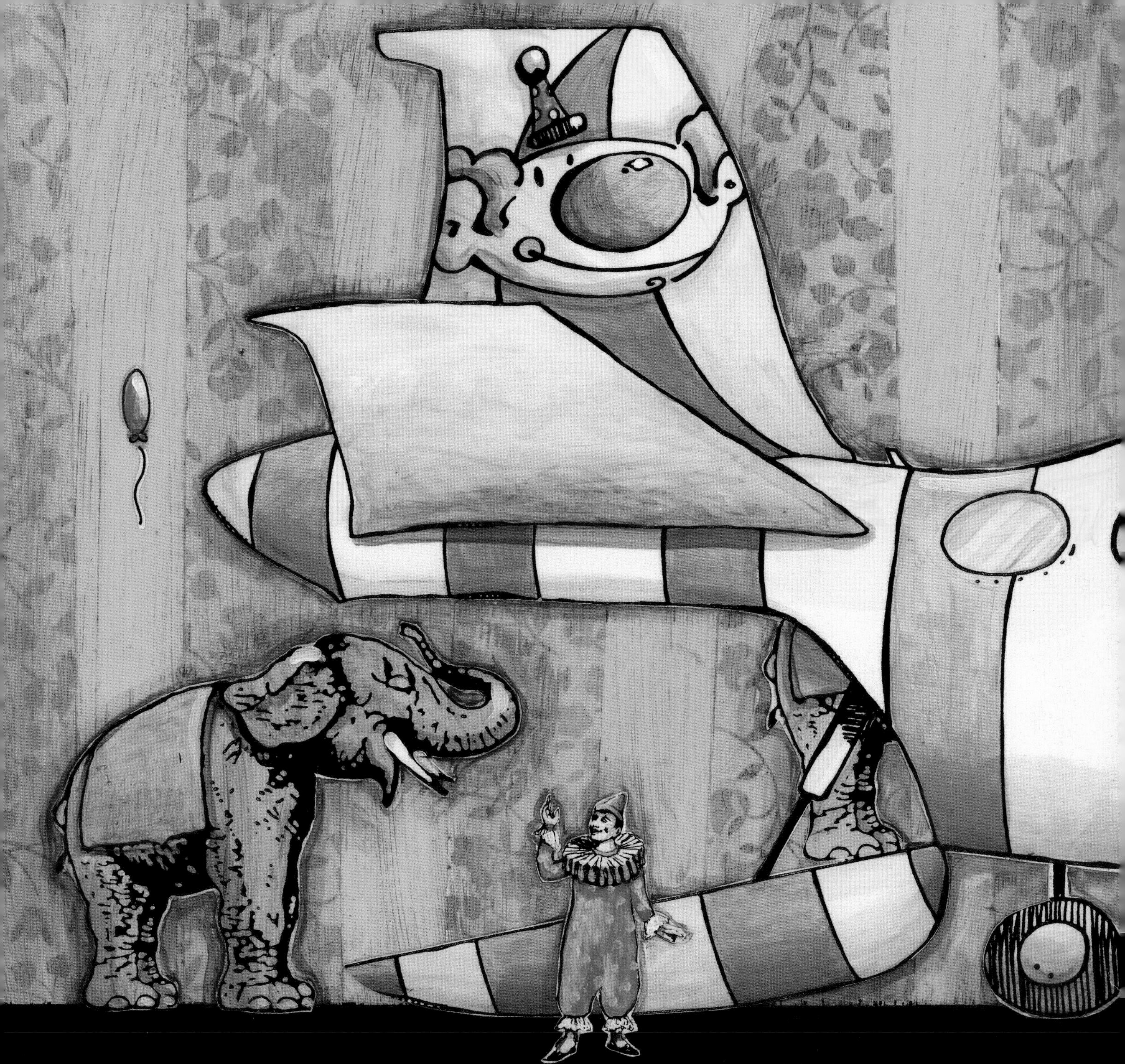

Fill them up and off they zoom!

Little planes take short,

quick

hops,

or dust a farmer's growing crops.

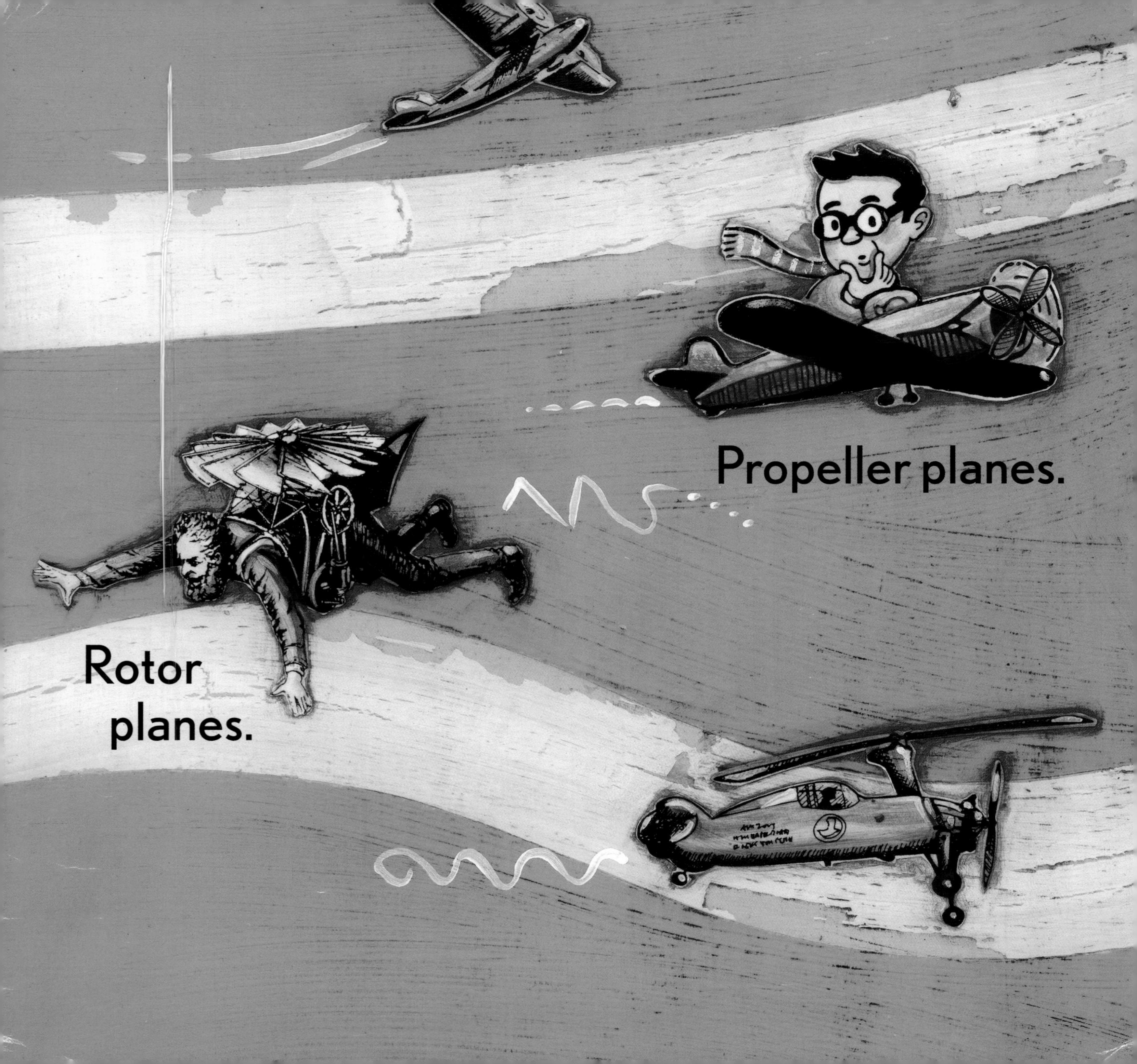

Propeller planes.

Rotor planes.

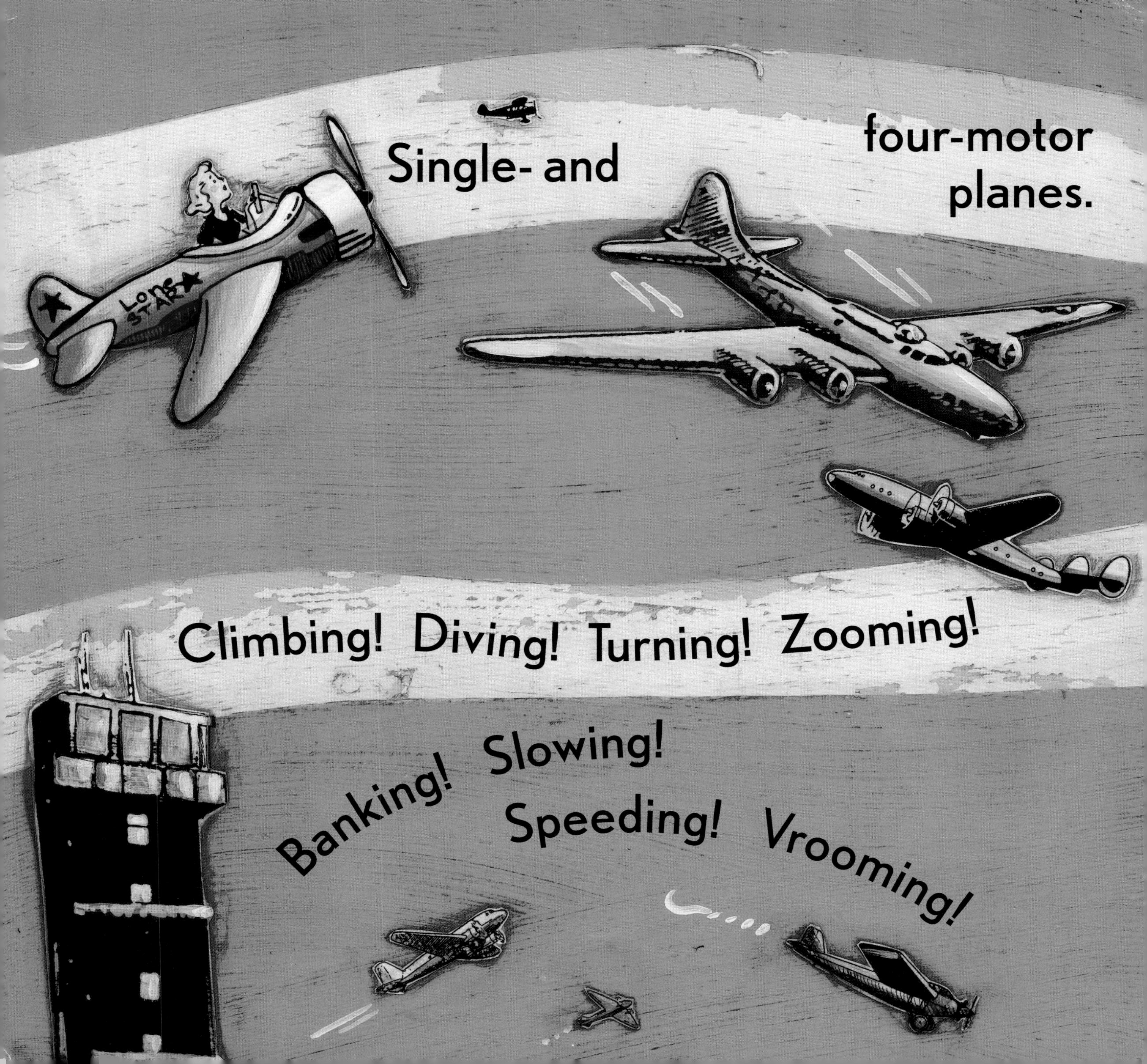
Single- and
four-motor
planes.
Lone STAR
Climbing! Diving! Turning! Zooming!
Banking! Slowing!
Speeding! Vrooming!

Planes fly in tight formation,
saluting heroes of each nation.

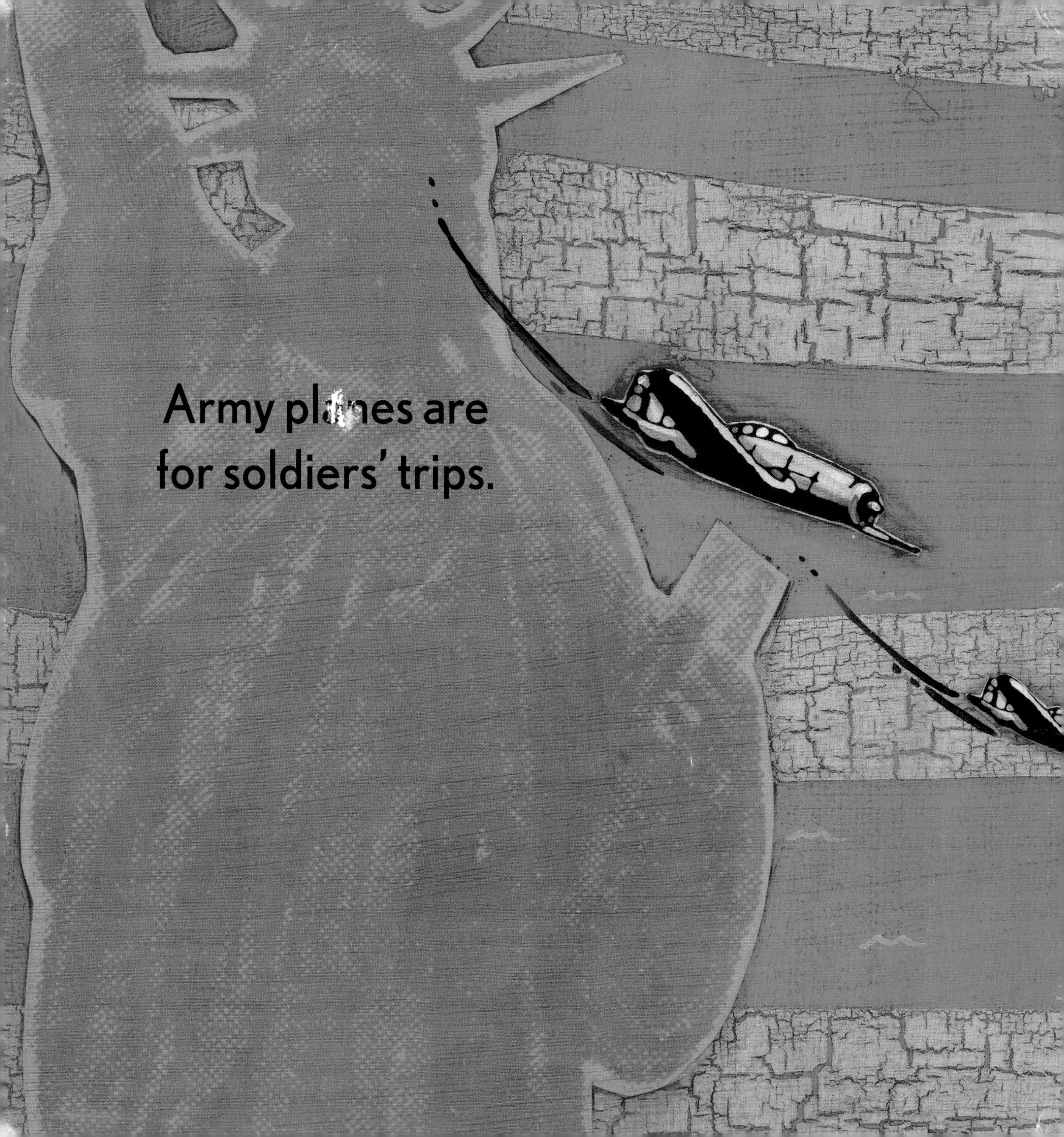

Army planes are
for soldiers' trips.

Navy planes can land on ships.

Air show planes loop and roll—

daring pilots in control!

Dare-Devil Dog Air Show
Dare-Devil Dog Air Show

Hydroplanes land at sea.

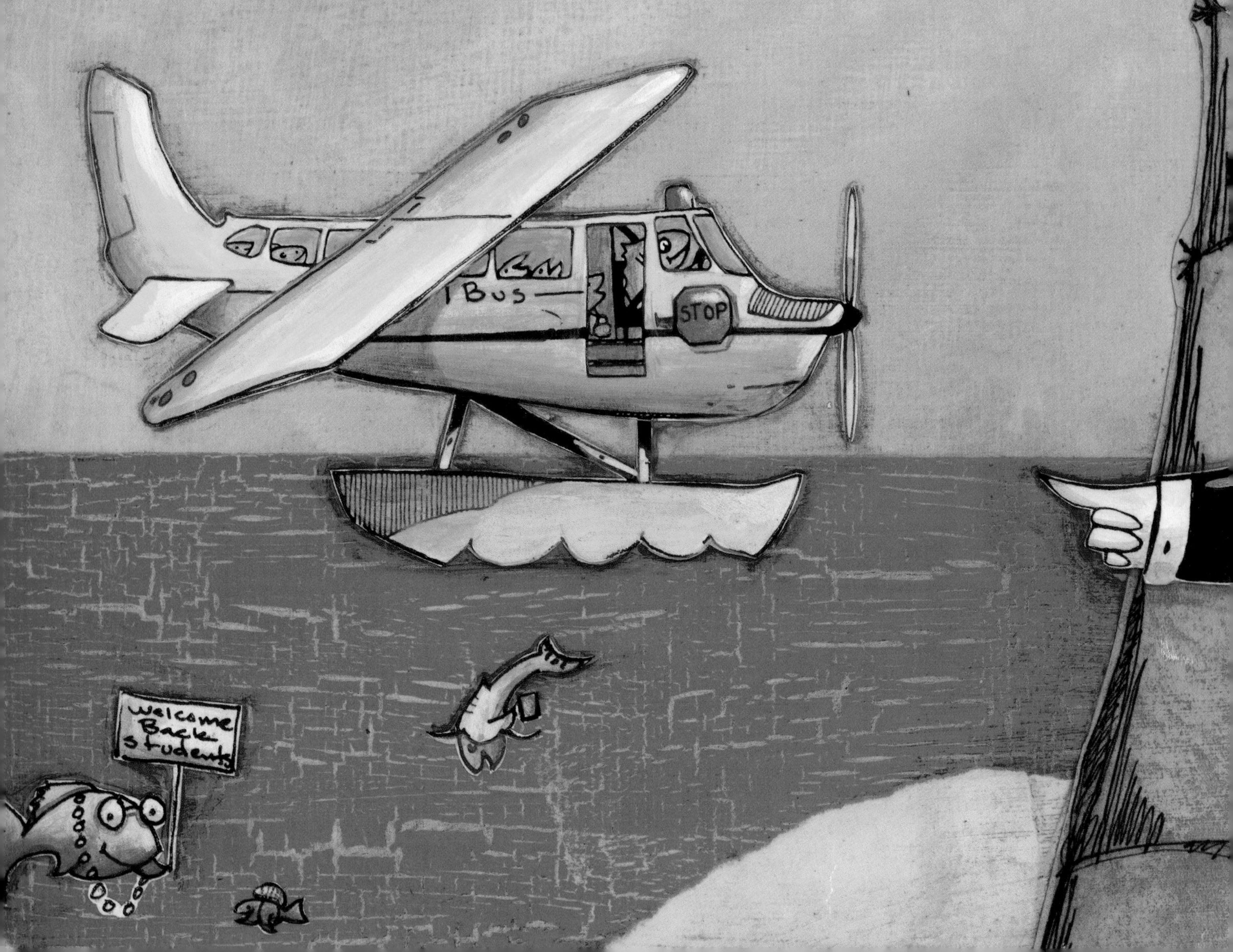

Planes bring us pictures on TV.

Jumbo jets hold packed-in crowds,

flying them high above the clouds.

Little planes flying low,

pull long banners as they go.

Planes, planes, planes,

in the big, wide sky!

Single-wing

and biplanes.

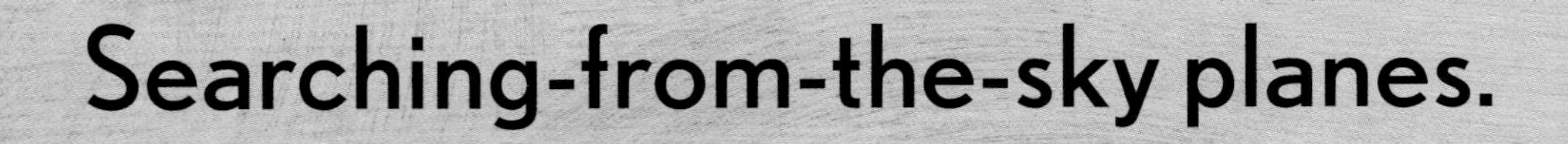

Searching-from-the-sky planes.

Mail planes.

Weather planes.

Bringing-us-together planes.

Model planes whiz and buzz,

circling like a big plane does.

Planes fly North,

South,

East,

and West.

They do their jobs.

N
E
S
LIBERTY
SUNNY SKIES AIRLINE

Then they rest.